How to Catch a MONSTER

Adam Wallace &
Andy Elkerton

sourcebooks
jabberwocky

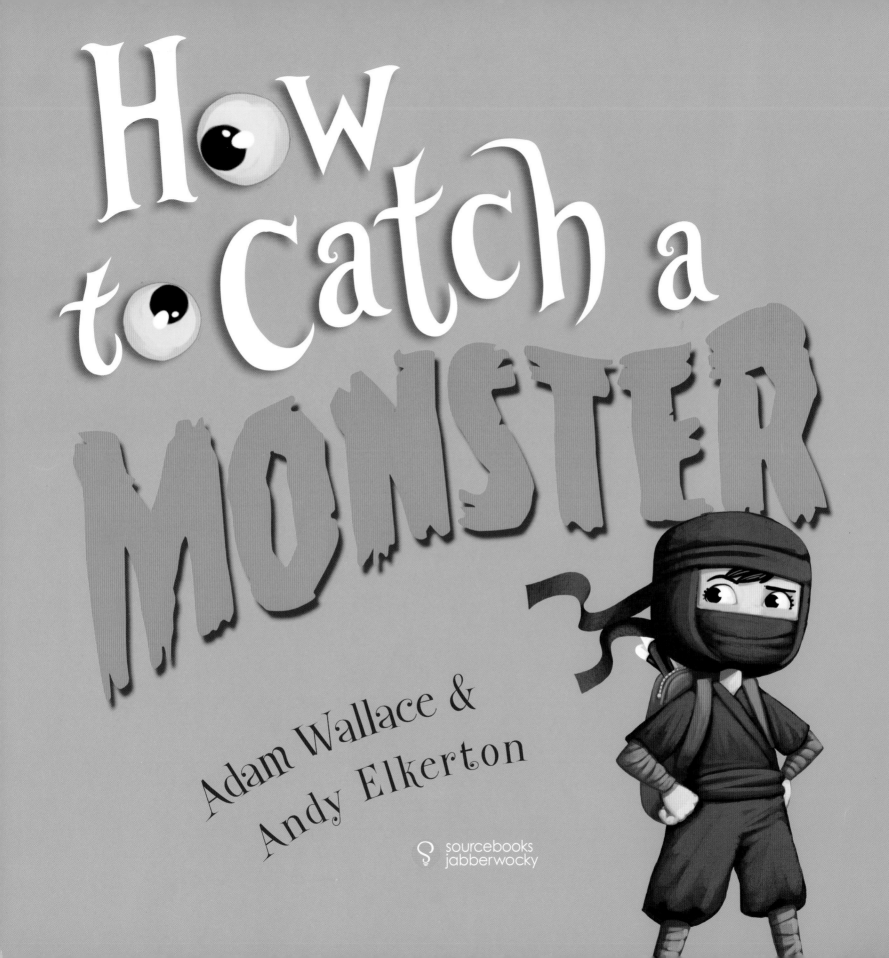

School is done, I'm heading home.

It was such an awesome day!

I got the role of NINJA MASTER

in this year's school play!

So now I'm feeling brave and strong,
and full of courage, too!
But if I'm going to be a HERO,
then there's one thing left to do!

How to be a NINJA

He lives just right through there...

I spot my monster right away.
He's practicing his ROAR.
He almost scares me half to death,
but I won't be scared anymore!

I reach into my bag of tricks
and pull out my first trap.
I'll catch my monster right away.
It'll be a snap!

Okay, he's stronger than I thought.
But I'm not finished yet.
I'll catch him in my SUPER-STICKY
ninja-nabbing net!

Aack! He just ESCAPED again!
But my next trap will not miss.
I'll give him every trick I've got.
He won't get out of this!

I stare at him, and he stares back.
His monster eyes look sad.
"I'm sorry, friend. I really am.
Oh, please, just don't be mad."

"I never meant to scare you.

I did it by mistake.

It's hard to play when you're asleep.

I want you **wide awake!**"

So then I stop my **NINJA BOT**,
and he pulls the bars apart.
I shake his hand, and then he smiles...

"That's how we say hello, my friend.
We do it all the time!
Just take a whiff! You'll see it smells
like **strawberries** and **lime**."

And then he takes me to his house,
which seems a little weird.

He lets me meet his mom and dad.
Is this the **creature** that I feared?

We play for hours, and have such fun,
and eat Volcano Pie!
And when he throws me in the air,
he throws me really high!

Then, at last, it's time for bed.

He helps me brush my teeth.

But he squeezes all my toothpaste out...

he's strong beyond belief!

The night is done, and Mom comes in
to tuck me nice and tight.
I'm glad I'm feeling *safe and sound*.
It's time to say good night.

Copyright © 2017 by Sourcebooks, Inc.
Cover design by Sourcebooks, Inc.
Cover and internal illustrations © Andy Elkerton

Sourcebooks and the colophon are registered trademarks of Sourcebooks, Inc.

Published by Sourcebooks Jabberwocky, an imprint of Sourcebooks, Inc.
P.O. Box 4410, Naperville, Illinois 60567-4410
(630) 961-3900
Fax: (630) 961-2168
www.sourcebooks.com

Library of Congress Cataloging-in-Publication data is on file with the publisher.

Source of Production: Leo Paper, Heshan City, Guangdong Province, China
Date of Production: May 2017
Run Number: 5009401

Printed and bound in China.

LEO 10 9 8 7 6 5 4 3 2 1